We prepare the earth with care.

We plant our seeds and hope.

We tend our garden and watch

Tomorrow's fruits and flowers grow.

Our School GARDEN!

by Rick Swann • illustrated by Christy Hale

Readers to Eaters
Bellevue, Washington

FIRST DAY

New city, new school,
No friends, and all alone.

Mr. Roberts leans to shake my hand.
"You must be Michael. Welcome!
Jesse will give you a tour."

He shows me the library, office, nurse,
Lunchroom, art, and gym.
"The best is last." He grins. "Out here!"

I open double doors expecting
Playfields, courts, or jungle gyms
But stop in place, amazed.

By what? A living space
With vibrant greens, fruits and flowers
And hum of bees . . .

Our school garden!

cauliflower

cabbage

onions

peas

rhubarb

We prepare the earth with care.
We plant our seeds and hope.
We tend our garden and watch
Tomorrow's fruits and flowers grow.

3 Sisters

I'm paired with Julie, who reads
"Find a leaf you want to eat!"

We wander through the garden.
So many kinds of leaves,
And Julie knows them all—
Chard, collards, lettuce,
Arugula, mustard, and kale.

"Which do you like best?" she asks.
"I've had lettuce, I guess,
But I don't know the rest."

"Do you like spicy, sour, sweet?"
"Spicy," I say.
Mama tells me you've got to
Have some spice in life.
Julie hands me a mustard leaf.
Nice and tangy hot.

"Time's up," I hear Mr. Roberts say.
Already? No way!
"Welcome to the garden, Michael."

collards

lettuce

arugula

kale

chard

mustard

A school garden is a
wonderful place to learn about
the environment and our local food system.
But did you know that it's also a great place to explore
science, math, social studies, art, and writing? A garden can
be as small as a few containers of soil or as large as a playfield.
All you need is an idea and some dedication. Let's get started!

THE
ENORMOUS
CARROT

I see you growing in our garden bed—
Long, feathery leaves.
"A weed!" I declare. Jesse agrees,
So I try to pull you out.

You won't budge!
"Help me pull!" I shout to Shannon.
Then I reach down for another tug
As Shannon tugs on me.

"It still won't budge!" I shout again,
So Jesse lends a hand.
But in the end we need Julie, too,
To finally yank you free.

After tumbling down we all laugh
At the surprising way
We learned today
That carrots grow underground!

Did you know that we eat all different parts of plants? Carrots are roots of plants and grow underground. Peas grow in pods that hang from vines, but peanuts grow as underground pods. We eat the leaves of many plants, such as spinach and lettuce. When we eat celery and rhubarb, we eat the stalks, not the leaves. Have you ever eaten an artichoke? It's a flower!

SCHOOL GARDEN STONE SOUP

Serves 25-30

Ingredients

4 cups dried beans   6 cups roots

8 quarts stock   3 cups greens

herbs   salt

1 cleaned rock   (an adult to help)

Directions

Soak the smooth, stone-hard
Beans overnight.
They'll drink and swell.
Then pour off the water.

Move the beans to a giant pot.
Add the stock, the herbs, and the rock.
Simmer for 90 minutes
Or until the beans are soft.

Now add the cut-up roots
(Potatoes, turnips, carrots).
Cook for half an hour
Or until they turn just tender.

Next, chop the leafy greens
And add them to the pot.
Simmer for 10 minutes,
Then add some salt to taste.

Last, find a group of friends
And a bowl and spoon for each
To taste the most delicious soup
We bet they'll ever eat!

"**S**tone Soup" is a folk tale
about sharing food. Did you know that
eating with others is actually good for you?
When sharing meals, people tend to slow down
their eating, which allows time for the stomach to tell
the brain when it's full. (It takes about 20 minutes.)
One more thing: Kids who eat with their families
tend to get better grades in school.

HARVEST DAY!

So much to see and do!
Salsa making, face painting,
Pumpkin carving, cider pressing,
Even Mr. Roberts dancing!

Eating foods that families brought—
Kimchi, curried peas,
Frybread, stir-fry,
Collard greens and apple pie.

But nothing is as good to eat
As what we cooked in class—
School garden stone soup
Made from what we grew.

When it's time for us to sing
Our garden song, I see
My parents clap their hands
And sing along.

"We prepare the earth with care.
We plant our seeds and hope.
We tend our garden and watch
Tomorrow's fruits and flowers grow."

This is the best day ever since I moved.
Maybe my best day ever, too.

Harvest time is celebrated by many cultures. These festive events, such as American Thanksgiving, Jewish Sukkoth, Chinese Moon Festival, and Indian Pongal, often include special foods and customs. Harvest Day at school is a fun way to celebrate seasonal foods and the hard work of students, teachers, and parents.

PILL BUGS

Julie yells, "Potato bug!"
Shannon shouts out, "Cheese log!"
Jesse bellows, "Doodlebug!"
And Simon grunts, "Chucky pig."

We search the garden
Where you lurk
Under logs and rocks,
Leaves and sticks.

And when I find you,
I cry out, too.
"Roly-poly,
Garden pill!"

The woodlouse has many crazy names. *Sow bug*, *slater*, *gramersow*, *butcher boy*, and *carpenter* are a few more. A wood louse is fun to watch, because it can curl itself into an armored ball like a miniature armadillo. This helpful creature creates rich soil by eating dead plants and pooping out important nutrients—little pills for your garden!

HOMONYM: ONE WORD, MANY MEANINGS

Jesse and I carry boxes of garden vegetables
Down the block to the food bank.

Julie and Shannon bank the garden beds with leaves
Before winter weather brings us snowbanks.

Mr. Roberts draws money from our bank account
To pay for seed-bank seeds.

Let's hope cloud banks bring spring rains,
As we're banking on a great growing year!

The word *bank* is a homonym,
a word that can have different
meanings but is pronounced the
same way. A bank is a place where
things are held for future use:
seed bank, food bank, or bank
for money. Bank can mean
to create a pile of something,
such as to bank mulch, or
to be a piled-up mass, such as
a snowbank. Many schools
donate their food to
local food banks.
Bank on that!

We Eat because we Work

We belong to the—
U.S. School Garden Army

HAVE A

Victory Garden

Eat what you can, and
can what you can't eat

FOUND POEM

The garden sleeps in winter
But not our class.
We learn about victory gardens

By studying war posters from the past.
I use their slogans
For my "found poem":

We eat because we work.
Grow vitamins at your kitchen door.

Eat what you can
And can what you can't.

Raised 'em myself in my U.S. school garden.
Grow for it!

During World War I and II, the United States government encouraged people to grow food in victory gardens at homes and schools so that food from farms could go to soldiers abroad. In 2009, with the help of schoolchildren, First Lady Michelle Obama created a victory garden at the White House as a way to promote healthy eating.

GARDEN RIDDLES

1.
I am the plant's beginning,
I am hidden away, black in red.

2.
I have many eyes
But never see.

3.
Gobble me up—
I am red meat!

4.
Cousin to cabbage,
I have a long body
And many green heads.

5.
Pick me and you're fine.
Open me up and you cry.

COMPOST

The compost warms my hands
As my cold fingers wriggle
Into the crumbly mix
Like fat, burrowing worms.

We share the shoveling
On this cold, crisp day,
Our steaming breath
Blending with the compost steam.

We work like dogs—
No! We work like worms
To make the black gold
That turns garden soil rich.

Something is rotten in your garden, and you should be glad! It's your compost pile: a mix of decaying leaves, vegetable scraps, and other plant materials. It is nature's way of recycling. You need to turn over the pile regularly to make the best compost. Compost is so good for your soil it's sometimes called "black gold."

We have so tenderly cared for you: sowing your seeds, watering your soil, providing your light and measuring your growth. But you've outgrown your pots. Now it is time for you to go forth, to set your roots deep in rich earth, to reach up toward the sunlight and bear fruit.

Don't wait until the ground gets warm to plant seeds!
Many schools grow baby plants indoors in the late
winter and then host a spring plant sale to raise
money for seeds and other garden supplies.
Some schools grow extra seedlings to
share with community organizations
that help low-income families.
Why not do both?

THREE SISTERS

"I wish I had a sister," I tell Simon
As I slowly mound the earth.

We crater the hilltops to hold water,
Then we begin to bury our seeds.

Sister corn, I place in the center.
She'll stand tall for support.

Sister squash, Julie plants at the edge.
She'll protect the soil and roots.

Beans, Simon puts between her sisters.
She'll hug them both as she climbs toward the sun.

Planting them together is "companion planting,"
Like Julie and Simon and me!

The three sisters—corn, squash, and beans—
were the most important crops for many
Native American diets. In companion planting,
they are planted together so that corn can
give support to the bean vines, and the beans
can put nitrogen in the soil to help the corn
grow. Squash protects the roots of the other
plants and cuts down on weeds. That is one
happy—and delicious—family!

LAST DAY OF SCHOOL!

Jesse likes the tomatoes best.
Julie loves the flowers.

Shannon trails the butterflies.
Simon loves to dig.

In art we sit and look
Long before we paint.

In science we test to see
What roly polies eat.

In math we weigh and graph
Our harvest for the week.

And in health we cook and eat
Roots and zesty greens.

Me, what I love best
Is to be outside with friends

In our school garden!

A school garden is even better than a playground. You can get your hands dirty digging, sit quietly and observe a butterfly, or enjoy being outside with your friends—during class time, not recess! If you don't have a garden at your school, it's time to talk to your teachers and parents, and to gather your friends to create one. Don't wait. Grow for it!

Author's Note

I first started researching school gardens when I became the librarian at Bagley Elementary in Seattle. The school was in the process of reviving an old, underused garden. I found a vintage photo of a huge elementary school garden filled with children working in it. Frank Cooper, the head of the Seattle school system at the time, said gardening was important because "the child studies THINGS . . . not through the eyes of the textbooks, but through his own."

In 1906, the year my school opened, there were about 75,000 school gardens in the United States. In 1914 the U.S. Bureau of Education created the Office of School and Home Gardening. In 1917 the War Department got into the act by funding the School Garden Army: "A garden for every child, every child in a garden."

Why were there so many school gardens? Some people were worried that children were losing touch with nature because more and more families were moving from the countryside to the cities. Educators at the time, including John Dewey and Maria Montessori, believed that children learned best with real-life experiences and activities. They also felt that lessons learned in the garden were more powerful than those read out of books or off a blackboard.

School gardens at the time were used to teach many subjects. For math, students had to calculate the cost and number of seeds needed to plant a bed. For writing, they wrote business correspondence to the seed company to order the seeds. For science, they measured the seeds' germination rate. For geography, they traced the origin and history of plants. And the garden's produce? It often fed local families in need.

In reviving our school garden, we echo those century old lessons. We follow the guideline: "Nature is our teacher." We want our students to know about and celebrate the cycles of life. We believe that the garden is a classroom that provides real-life lessons in observation, experimentation, and thought.

We are also concerned, like First Lady Michelle Obama, that children are not eating enough healthy foods and staying active. So we created a place where children can experience growing and eating their own food and be physically active producing it. We believe the garden can be a community gathering place that encourages cooperation and sharing. Finally, children can learn about helping others by donating fresh food from our garden to the local food bank.

The resources I provide here can give you, your parents, and your teachers ideas of what to do in the garden. A lot of these activities are fun to do on your own at home as well, and some don't even need a garden space! Growing bulbs indoors, for instance, is an easy project that can brighten your winter.

I would encourage you to read more about gardening. Some of my favorites storybooks are *The Curious Garden* by Peter Brown and *Weslandia* and *Seedfolks* by Paul Fleischman. A great book

that connects what we eat with the environment is *Reducing Your Foodprint* by Ellen Rodger. There are also lots of fun gardening books, such as *Roots, Shoots, Buckets & Boots* and *Sunflower Houses* by Sharon Lovejoy.

One of my favorite garden quotations is from the book *How to Grow a School Garden:* "School gardens are, in fact, libraries full of life, mystery, and surprise." Being in a garden is like reading a good book: You're never sure what is on the next page, but you can't wait to get there and find out. So what are you waiting for?

Resources

How to Grow a School Garden: A Complete Guide for Parents and Teachers by Arden Bucklin-Sporer and Rachel Kathleen Pringle is a wonderful reference if you are interested in starting a garden at your school.

Edible Schoolyard: A Universal Idea by Alice Waters is a book that details the mission and history of the gardening and cooking program at Martin Luther King Middle School in Berkeley, California. The program's website (www.edibleschoolyard.org) offers useful supplemental information and material.

City Bountiful by Laura J. Lawson gives an overview of community and school gardening in the United States from the 1890s to the present. Most of the reasons school gardens were encouraged a hundred years ago are applicable today.

School Garden Wizard (www.schoolgardenwizard.org) was created through a partnership between the United States Botanic Garden and Chicago Botanic Garden. It makes a great case for creating, using, maintaining, and evaluating a school garden.

One of the National Gardening Association's websites, www.kidsgardening.org, is rich with ideas for gardening with children. This site also maintains a national registry of school gardens.

California has championed a garden in every school for years. The California School Garden Network's comprehensive website is www.csgn.org.

Life Lab (www.lifelab.org) offers environmental, hands-on science and garden-based programs. They publish *The Growing Classroom: Garden-Based Science*, one of the best garden-based curriculum guides available.

Acknowledgments

I could not have written this book without the support of the school-garden advocates who allowed me to interview them and, in some cases, to tour their school gardens. Thank you to Erin MacDougall, Tricia Kovacs, Joan A. Qazi, Mary Warren, Cheri Bloom, Anthony Warner, Michael Dempster, Karen Ray, Michelle Ratcliffe, Marcela Abadi, Carol Barker, Janet Nielsen-Homan, Kyle Andersen, and Marguerite Humphrey.

To Carlyn, my dirt mover—R.S.

For Scott and Kate—C.H.

Rick Swann is a school librarian in Seattle, Washington. He has been a gardener since he was four, picking asparagus and blueberries near his childhood home in New England. Now he harvests vegetables with his students from their school garden for the local food bank. He lives in Seattle with his wife, Carlyn. This is his first book. Learn more about Rick at www.rickswann.com.

Christy Hale has illustrated many award-winning picture books, including *Elizabeti's Doll* and its two sequels. She is also the author and illustrator of *The East-West House: Noguchi's Childhood in Japan*, named a Best Book of the Year by *Kirkus Reviews*. When she is not making books, she's busy making marmalade and lemonade from her grapefruit, orange, and lemon trees at her home in Palo Alto, California. Learn more about Christy at www.christyhale.com.

Text copyright © 2012 by Rick Swann
Illustrations copyright © 2012 by Christy Hale

READERS to EATERS Books
12437 SE 26th Place, Bellevue, WA 98005
Distributed by Publishers Group West

www.ReadersToEaters.com
Follow us on Facebook and Twitter

Printed in U.S.A. by Worzalla, Stevens Point, Wisconsin (2/12)

FSC
www.fsc.org
MIX
Paper from
responsible sources
FSC® C002589

Book design by Christy Hale
Book production by The Kids at Our House
The text is set in P22 Stanyan and Triplex Serif
The art is done in mixed media, combining collaged papers, stencils, printing, and paint.

10 9 8 7 6 5 4 3 2 1
First Edition

Cataloging-in-Publication Data is on file at the Library of Congress ISBN 978-0-9836615-0-4

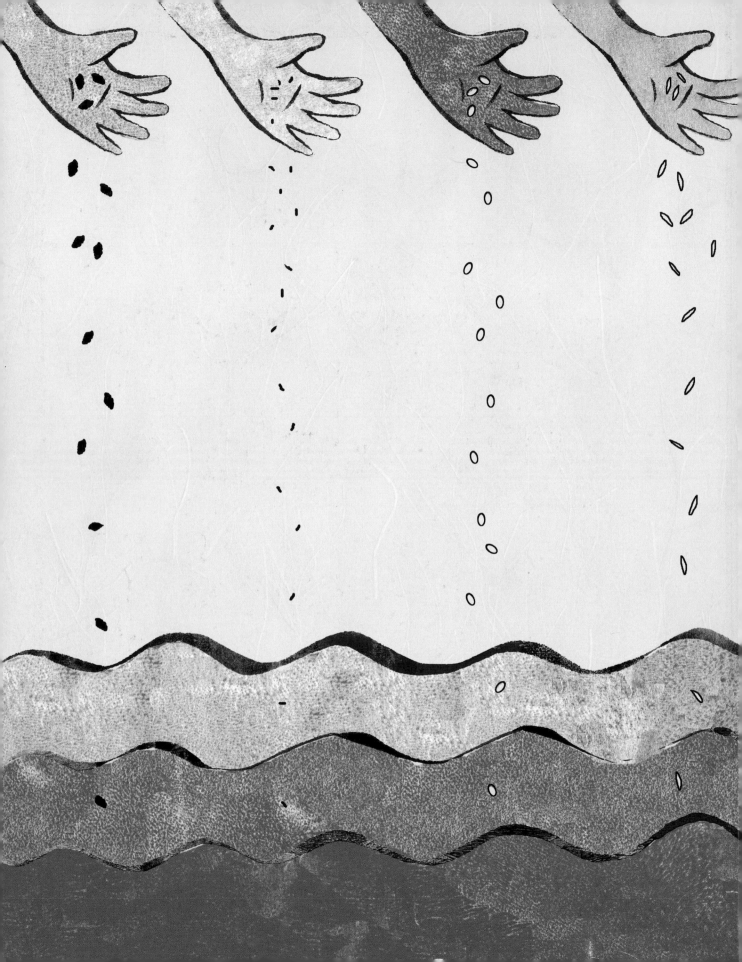